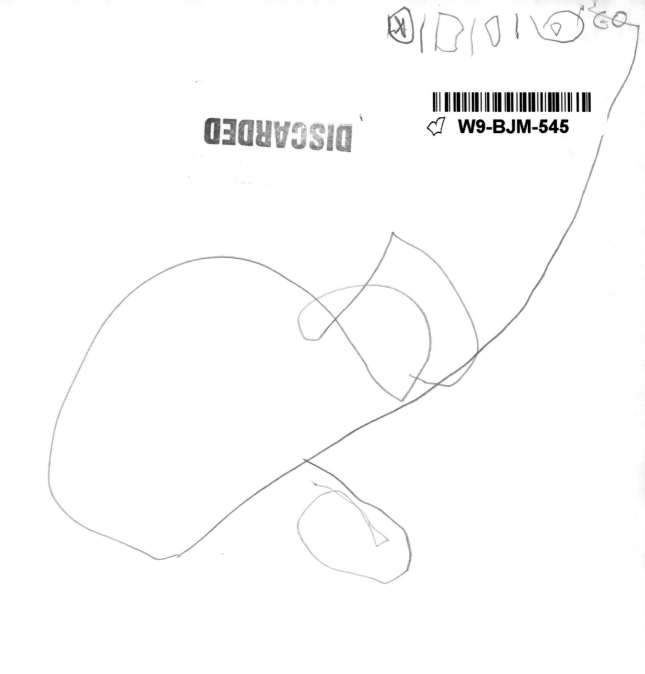

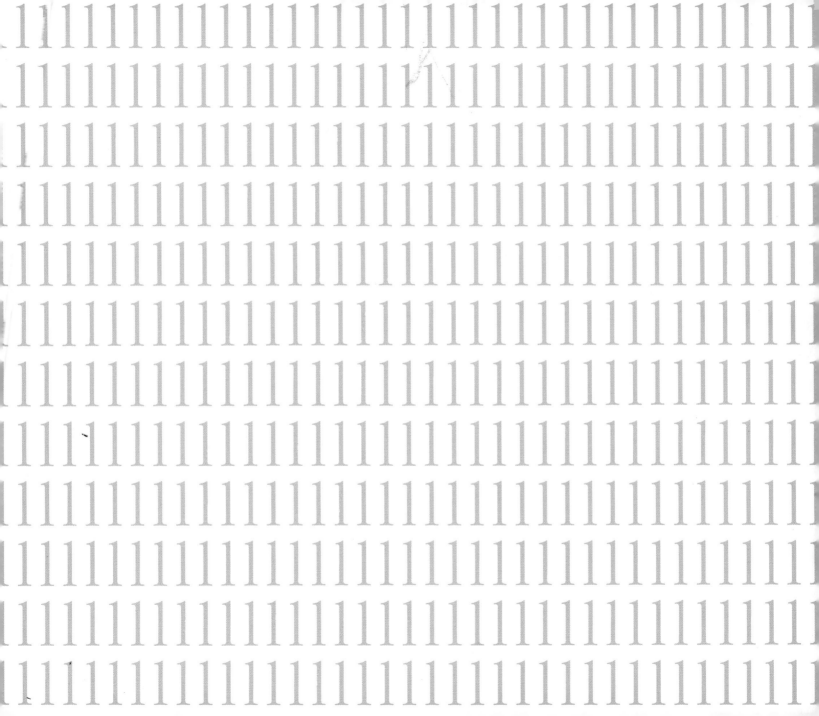

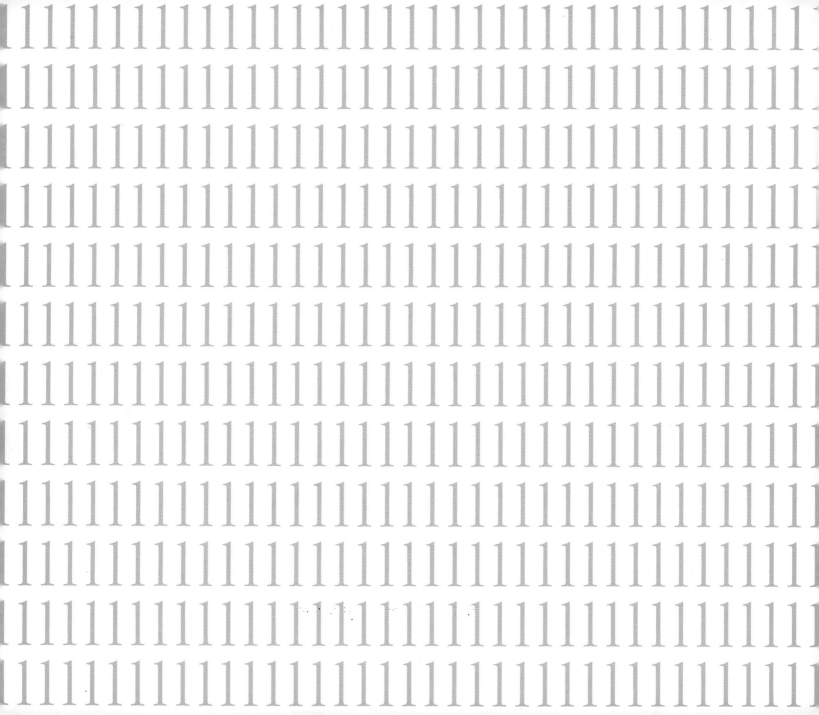

My "l" Sound Box®

Library of Congress Cataloging-in-Publication Data
Moncure, Jane Belk.
My "l" sound box / by Jane Belk Moncure; illustrated by Colin King.
p. cm.
Summary: A little boy fills his sound box with many words beginning with the letter "l."
ISBN 1-56766-778-3 (lib. bdg. : alk. paper)
[1. Alphabet.] I. King, Colin, ill. II. Title.
PZ7.M739 Myl   2000
[E]—dc21   99-055422

My "l"
Sound Box®

Jane Belk Moncure
illustrated by Colin King

The Child's World®

Little  had a box.

"I will find things that begin
with my 'l' sound," he said.

"I will put them into my sound  box."

Little 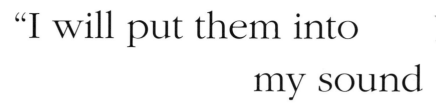 looked under the leaves and found lizards.

Did he put the leaves and the lizards into his box? He did.

Then Little  looked behind some

logs

and found lambs.

They were little lambs.

"You must be lost," said Little 1.

So he put the little lambs
and the logs into the box
with the leaves and the lizards.

Then Little  walked to a lake.

The lizards leaped out of the box.

But Little  put them back.

"I do not like leaping lizards," he said.

Little 1 looked in the lake and found a lobster.

He lifted the lobster into the box . . .
carefully . . .

because the lobster had long claws.

Then Little 1 saw a lighthouse by the lake.

He went inside
the lighthouse.
The lantern
was not on.

So Little climbed up the
ladder . . .

and lit the

lantern.

"Someone may be lost," he said.

Little  heard a loud roar.

He opened the door and found a little

 lion.

The little lion licked him.

The little lion sat in his lap.

He gave the lion a lollipop.

"You must be lost," he said.
"You belong in my sound box."

Little  heard another loud roar.
He opened the door

and found a little leopard.

The little leopard
licked him.

The little leopard
sat in his lap.

Little gave the leopard a lollipop.

"You must be lost," he said.

       "You belong in my box, too."

But when he put the little leopard
into the box . . .

the lobster pinched the leopard's leg.
The leopard leaped.

Then the lion leaped.

The lambs leaped,

and the lizards leaped, too.

So Little  put the lobster

into a lobster cage.

Just then, he heard another loud roar.

He opened the door and saw

a locomotive.

"Let's go for a long ride!" he said.

lobster in lobster cage

logs and ladder

leaves and lizards

leopard licking lollipop

lion and lambs

locomotive

And they did.

Can you read these words with Little 1 ?

lamp

letter

lime

light

lemon

lovebirds

ladybug

lace

28

lettuce

llama

lark

lady

lock

lily

lifeguard

ABOUT THE AUTHOR AND ILLUSTRATOR

Jane Belk Moncure began her writing career when she was in kindergarten. She has never stopped writing. Many of her children's stories and poems have been published, to the delight of young readers, including her son Jim, whose childhood experiences found their way into many of her books.

Mrs. Moncure's writing is based upon an active career in early childhood education. A recipient of an M.A. degree from Columbia University, Mrs. Moncure has taught and directed nursery, kindergarten, and primary grade programs in California, New York, Virginia, and North Carolina. As a former member of the faculties of Virginia Commonwealth University and the University of Richmond, she taught prospective teachers in early childhood education.

Mrs. Moncure has travelled extensively abroad, studying early childhood programs in the United Kingdom, The Netherlands, and Switzerland. She was the first president of the Virginia Association for Early Childhood Education and received its award for outstanding service to young children.

A resident of North Carolina, Mrs. Moncure is currently a full-time writer and educational consultant. She is married to Dr. James A. Moncure, former vice president of Elon College.

Colin King studied at the Royal College of Art, London. He started his freelance career as an illustrator, working for magazines and advertising agencies.

He began drawing pictures for children's books in 1976 and has illustrated over sixty titles to date.

Included in a wide variety of subjects are a best-selling children's encyclopedia and books about spies and detectives.

His books have been translated into several languages, including Japanese and Hebrew. He has four grown-up children and lives in Suffolk, England, with his wife, three dogs, and a cat.

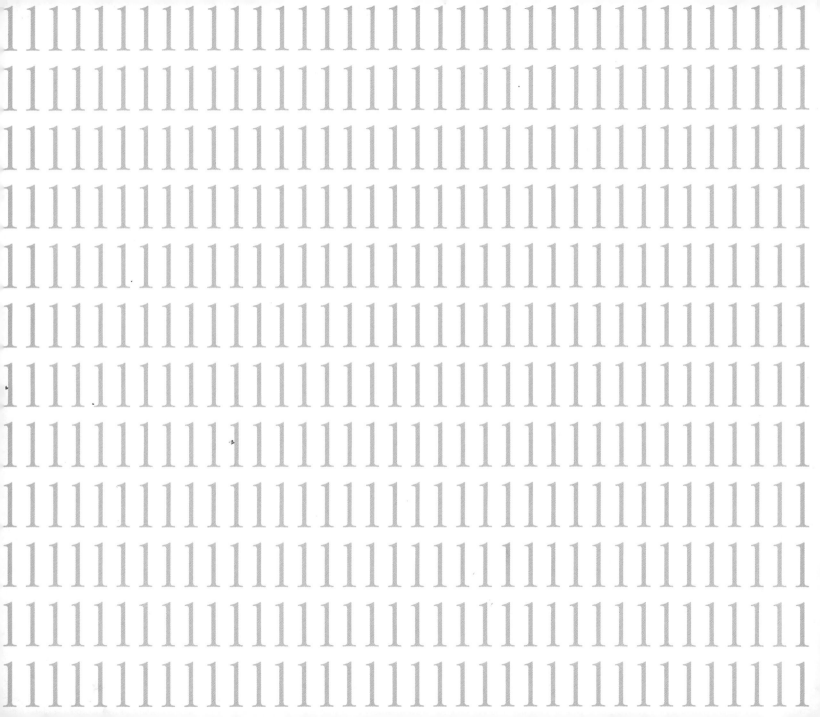